Copyright © 2007 by NordSüd Verlag AG, Zürich, Switzerland
First published in Switzerland under the title *Ein Weihnachtsfest für den Bären*
English translation copyright © 2007 by North-South Books Inc., New York

First published in the United States, Great Britain, Canada, Australia, and New Zealand in 2007
by North-South Books Inc., an imprint of NordSüd Verlag AG, Zürich, Switzerland.
Distributed in the United States by North-South Books Inc., New York.

Library of Congress Cataloging-in-Publication Data is available.
A CIP catalogue record for this book is available from The British Library.
ISBN-13: 978-0-7358-2145-3 / ISBN-10: 0-7358-2145-3 (trade edition)

10 9 8 7 6 5 4 3 2 1

Printed in Belgium

www.northsouth.com

The Rabbit and the Bear

A Christmas Tale

By Ivan Gantschev

Translated by J. Alison James

NORTHSOUTH
BOOKS
New York / London

IT WAS THE DAY BEFORE CHRISTMAS and snow was everywhere. The world glittered in the sunlight. Two hunters walked out into the woods with their guns and their dogs. They hoped to find something special for their Christmas dinner. They carried provisions of bread, fruit, cheese, carrots, cakes, and a big jar of honey.

A rabbit was also out in the woods. He was excited about winter. This time of year was always so wonderfully peaceful and quiet. The only thing he had to watch out for was the fox. Or so he thought! Just then he heard a voice shout, "There! Look! A rabbit!"

Then came the thunder of a pair of hounds, barking and growling, following his scent.

Terrified, the rabbit flew across an open field. He ran as fast as he could. But the hounds were faster. Soon they were so close, he could hear them panting!

With his last bit of strength, the rabbit reached the woods, where the trees and rocks provided some cover. The rabbit took a huge leap, but the ground gave way beneath his feet. He fell and fell, finally landing—*pflump*—on something soft.

"Grrr," the softness growled.

The rabbit had landed on a bear, asleep in her cave. "I'm so sorry," he stammered. "I didn't mean to disturb you. But there are hounds out there, chasing me!"

The bear growled again. Then she stretched and forced her eyes open. "You woke me up from a strange dream," she said. She peered at the rabbit. She didn't look angry, just bewildered.

"Why don't you tell me your dream?" the rabbit suggested. He wanted to stay in the safety of the cave for as long as possible. So the bear began.

"I was far away, in a land without cold or snow. The land was full of orange trees and olive trees, with stony hills. I was following a woman and a man. They seemed to be searching for something. They looked tired. The sun was almost down when they found a stable and went inside."

"Inside I could see animals: some sheep, a
donkey, and an ox. For a long time, all was still.
Then I heard the cry of a newborn baby. Suddenly
everything lit up, almost as bright as day! High
above the stable roof, a great star shone down.
I felt its glow deep in my heart."

"An owl flapped down and perched next to me. Her eyes shone. 'We have witnessed a wonder,' she said. 'A child is born. He shall protect the poor and the weak.'"

The bear paused. "Isn't that strange?" she said to the rabbit, who listened attentively. "How can a tiny baby protect the weak? In the dream it made sense somehow, but now I just don't understand.

"Shepherds came with their sheep, just to see this child. Their faces were glowing with awe. Three noble men came on horses and camels, bringing the child splendid gifts. And all this time, the star shone down!

"I was on my way into the stable to see for myself, when you woke me from my dream. I wanted to see the child with my own eyes!" The bear shook herself.

"I am so sorry I woke you," said the rabbit. "You dreamt of the first Christmas! That was the birth of the baby Jesus a long, long time ago. Even now, people still gather to celebrate His birth. And today is Christmas Eve. You've had a Christmas dream!"

"I've never even heard of Christmas," said the bear. "Of course, I'm usually asleep this time of year." She shook herself again. "Now that I'm awake, I'm as hungry as a bear!"

"I might be able to find us something to eat," the rabbit said. "But it is too dangerous for me to go out alone, while the hunters are about. Would you come with me?"

The bear nodded. "Of course! I know nothing about Christmas, but if the owl in my dream was right, then it is no time for hunting. I promise you, today you will be safe!"

When the two animals emerged from the cave, they saw the hunters waiting with their dogs. The bear straightened up to her full height and took a few steps toward them, growling loudly.

Now it was the hunters' turn to be shocked! Since when were bears out in the winter? They took one frightened look and ran as fast as they could back to town.

All that was left behind were the bags filled with the hunters' provisions. The bear and the rabbit pulled the bags into the bear's cave and enjoyed a wonderful Christmas feast.

"Thank you," said the bear to the rabbit, when she had licked the last drop of honey from the jar. "I'm glad that you woke me. Now I know about Christmas, and the baby who protects the poor and the weak." She yawned loudly and curled up into a ball in the corner of her cave. "Good night," she said, and then she was sound asleep.

"Sweet dreams," whispered the rabbit. "I'll come visit in the spring." Then he slipped out of the cave into the deep dark woods. The stars above shone through the branches of the trees. "Merry Christmas!" he called to the trees and the stars. Then the little rabbit made his way back to his own warm bed for a deep midwinter sleep.